My New Skates

John Harvey

NEIGHBORHOOD READERS

Rosen Classroom Books & Materials™

New York

Alex wanted to go ice skating
with his friends.
"Mom, where are my skates?" asked Alex.
"Let's look for them," said Mom.

They looked in Alex's room.
"My skates are not here," said Alex.
"I will have to keep looking."

Pat came to see Alex.
"Let's go skating," said Pat.
"I can't find my skates," said Alex.
"I will help you look," said Pat.

4

They looked in the kitchen.
"My skates are not here," said Alex.
"See you later," said Pat.
"I have to go now."

Lisa came to see Alex.
"Let's go skating," said Lisa.
"I can't find my skates," said Alex.
"I will help you look," said Lisa.

6

They looked under the chair.
"My skates are not here," said Alex.
"Come to the skating rink when you find
the skates," said Lisa.

"Did you find your skates?" asked Mom.
"No," said Alex.
"Let's look for them outside," said Mom.

8

Mom and Alex looked in the car.
"My skates are not here," said Alex.
"Where can they be?"

"Maybe Mary has my skates," said Alex.
Alex and Mom went to Mary's house.
"I do not have your skates," said Mary.

10

"Let's go to the skating rink," said Mom.
"Maybe your skates are there."
"I hope I can find them," said Alex.

Alex saw his friends skating.
"I still can't find my skates," Alex said.
"Maybe we should go home."

"We can't go home yet," said Mom.
"We have something for you."
"We hope you like it," said Pat and Lisa.

"Happy birthday, Alex!" said Mom.
"Surprise!" said Lisa and Pat.
"What is in the box?" asked Alex.
"Open it," said Mom.

14

"I got new skates!" said Alex.
"Thanks, Mom!"
"Thanks, Lisa and Pat!"
"I like your new skates, Alex," said Pat.

Alex put on his new skates.
"I can't wait to skate!" said Alex.
"Have fun skating!" said Mom.